meow

meow

meow

meow

Stretch Goes for a Walk

Written and Illustrated
by Justin Beaton

A special thanks goes to Amy Beaton for proofreading and editing this book and Milani and Leo for coming to hang out with Stretch.

Dedicated to families everywhere who spend time with one another and love each other unconditionally the way God loves us. God Bless you all.

Stretch begins today's adventure by waking up and making pancakes. It's always good to thank God for waking us up each day and giving us food to eat.

Stretch knows that today is a special day. He has so much energy because he can hardly wait to find out what the big surprise is! He'll only have to wait a little bit longer.

Do you think he has any idea
what the surprise will be?

Let's find out if he knows.

Stretch loves his special
Kitty stroller because he
can experience the whole
world and be safe inside
at the same time.

He is so excited to see all
of God's creatures outside
in nature. I wonder what
we will see today.

Do you have any guesses?

But wait, there's another surprise! Stretch's cousins, Milani and Leo, are on their way over right now! Milani and Leo are so much fun, and they love going on adventures.

Milani and Leo love Stretch very much, and they want to make sure he's safe. They decide to start the walk by pushing the stroller together. God loves it when siblings share and get along.

Stretch is getting cozy inside his stroller. He has two windows that he can look out of—one big and one small. This way he doesn't miss any of the action.

Let's get going because we have a super fun adventure ahead!

Stretch gets his first look of the day at the trees and the sky.

He loves the cool wind and smelling all the scents in the air.

Cats have very powerful noses and can smell a lot of things that people can't.

I don't Know where we will end up or what things we will see. Let's Keep exploring! It looks like there are a lot of other people out walking today too.

We might be getting close to a park. I see some families over there. One has a kite and one has a dog.

It's Leo's turn to push
Stretch. He can choose
to take us wherever he
wants.

Stretch loves it when Leo pushes him in his stroller. They both look like they're having so much fun!

There's one thing I forgot to mention. Something special happens to each person who pushes Stretch in his special Kitty stroller.

It's happening to Leo right now...

Leo has taken us to Dino Land, and he has turned into a crazy dinosaur! Let's see how many dinos we can name.

DINO LAND

Dino Land is so much fun! Let's keep walking. Maybe Stretch's special kitty stroller has more surprises to come.

Hey wait, I think I see a city over there...

It's CrazyTown! Animals and Kids are driving in cars and flying in planes. I even see a dancing cheeseburger! When Leo pushes Stretch's Kitty stroller, we always end up in a fun and crazy place.

I can't believe we've already been to such neat places on our walk. It looks like there's a forest up ahead. It's Milani's turn to push Stretch in his stroller.

I wonder where Milani will take us...

Milani is very gentle with Stretch. She pushes him slow and steady. He can barely feel the bumps in the sidewalk because she does such a great job. She hasn't told us yet, but I think Milani has a secret fun place where she wants to go.

It's happening again! Let's see where
the special Kitty stroller will take us
now that Milani is pushing Stretch...

Look! Up ahead! It's a park where we can all play. It's Pretty Park! Let's walk over and look around.

There's going to be something special about Pretty Park, I just know it.

Look over to the left! It's a majestic field full of colorful flowers. God put a lot of beauty into his creation, don't you think? Let's run through the field!

Are you seeing what I'm seeing? It's a family of friendly foxes here to welcome us to Pretty Park! Let's say hello.

It's almost lunchtime, and we are all getting hungry. Let's head back home. It looks like some animals on the trail will help guide the way...

We finally made it back just in time for lunch. We had so much fun on our adventure today that Stretch needs to lie down and take a cat nap.

I hope that we can all take Stretch on another walk sometime very soon. If we do, we will probably see many more fun and interesting places—maybe even a few crazy ones.

Stretch's kitty stroller really is special. No wonder why he likes it so much!

But wait a second, where's Leo? He was just with us on the trail when we were walking home...

Leo is still outside! He must have wandered off to do some more exploring.

Maybe he was trying to go back to CrazyTown.

Or maybe he was trying to go back to Dino Land to ride a Pterodactyl!

It's a good thing Stretch learned how to drive a car when we were in CrazyTown. Milani had better wake him up so they can go get Leo and bring him home for lunch.

What a crazy guy Leo is!

Do you recognize any of these that
Leo saw in Dino Land or CrazyTown?

Hint: There are 6.

Hint: Go back and check pages 20-23 if you get stuck and can't remember.

Do you recognize any of these that Milani saw at Pretty Park?

Hint: There are 6.

Hint: Go back and check pages 28-35 if
you get stuck and can't remember.

Dear reader,

Thanks for coming along with us today on Stretch's walk. We learned about sharing with and caring for one another and saw much of God's beautiful creation.

Of all the things God made, the most special is you!

Did you know that you can read your Bible and talk to God every day by praying? That is how you have a relationship with Him. He loves you and wants to hear all about your day, even the smallest details. I hope you can join us for the next adventure with Stretch!

God Bless you,

Justin

JESUS L♥VES YOU

About the Author

Justin and his lovely wife, Amy, live in Wisconsin with the stretchiest feline that you ever did see. They are starting their family and can't wait to introduce their future kids to Stretch!

Credits

This book was designed in Canva in conjunction with Adobe Photoshop, Affinity Photo 2, and BeFunky. All visual assets are primarily from Justin Beaton (actual photos converted to illustrations) and Canva. Pages 6-7, and 32-33 were generated with Recraft AI and then edited. All story text was originally written by Justin Beaton and edited by Amy Beaton. A special thanks goes to SimplyKDP for the initial template inspiration as well as Astrid from Genesiz Designs for some very timely guidance.

Made in the USA
Monee, IL
19 December 2024

74824240R00026